MEET MACK

Pam Smith

To order additional copies of this book, contact:
Xlibris
844-714-8691
www.Xlibris.com
Orders@Xlibris.com

ISBN: Softcover   979-8-3694-1141-4
         Hardcover   979-8-3694-1142-1
         EBook   979-8-3694-1140-7

Print information available on the last page

Rev. date: 05/14/2024

I dedicate this book to my grandparents, Grammy and Daddy Guy & Mama-Bedie and Pop. Since my parents were divorced, I truly spent a lot of time with all of them. They inspired me to appreciate a grandparent's love and guidance. I also dedicate this book to my fourth grade students at Moody Elementary. I was teaching creative writing to them and wrote this book as I was modeling for them.

Since my parents were divorced, my sister and I spent a lot of time with our grandparents. I was fortunate to have the best grandparents on both sides of my family. When I was with my dad, Paula and I stayed with Grammy and Daddy Guy. When I was with Momma, we lived across the street from my other grandparents, Mama-Bedie and Pop.

During the summer of 1964, my dad took Paula and me to Disneyland. On the way home, Dad bought us a pet parrot. We were so excited because now we had a playmate for our pet chihuahua, Cha-Cha. The parrot's name was Mack and the previous owner suggested we keep the parrot's name since Mack was very familiar with it. Bringing the new pet home to Grammy's was so exciting.

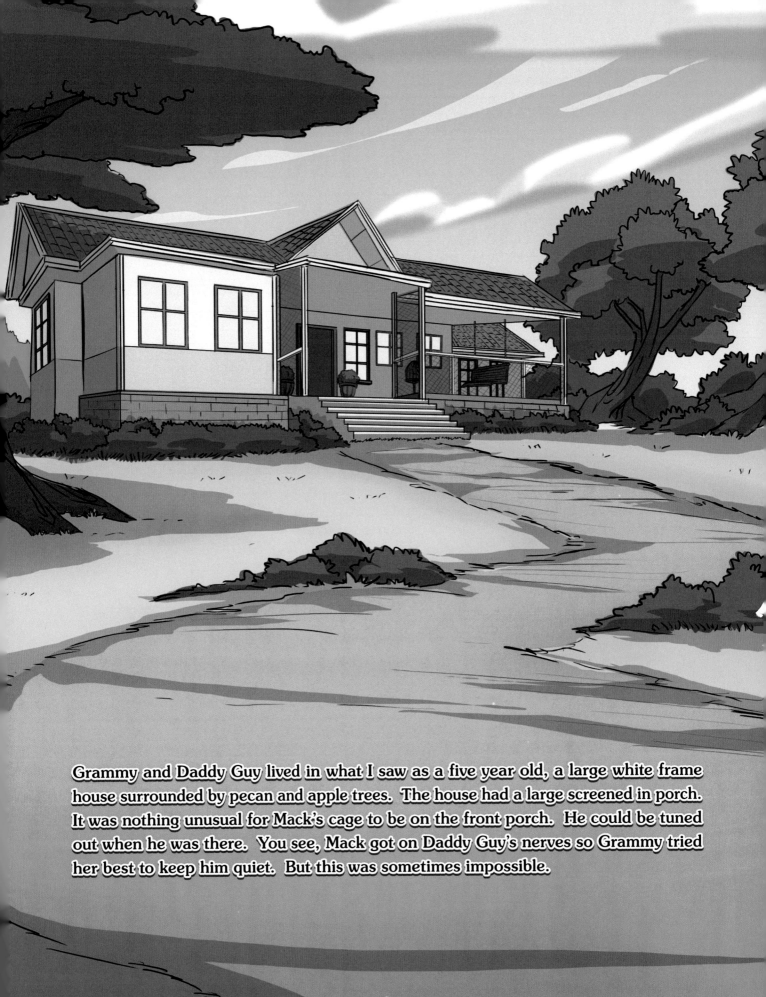

Grammy and Daddy Guy lived in what I saw as a five year old, a large white frame house surrounded by pecan and apple trees. The house had a large screened in porch. It was nothing unusual for Mack's cage to be on the front porch. He could be tuned out when he was there. You see, Mack got on Daddy Guy's nerves so Grammy tried her best to keep him quiet. But this was sometimes impossible.

Mack was quite a character and was always antagonizing Cha-Cha. "Can't you talk boy?" cried Mack. I bet Cha-Cha wanted to eat that bird.

"I'm hungry, Mack want a cracker! Grammy, Mack want a cracker!" yelled Mack to Grammy.

"In a minute, Mack," replied Grammy. She was forever waiting on Mack. She even fed him ice cream. In fact, she pampered and spoiled both Mack and Cha-Cha. Grammy quickly became Mack's favorite. Grammy was patient with Mack, but she was the only one patient with him. Daddy Guy, on the other hand, had no tolerance for Mack.

"Ahhh shut up, boy!" Daddy Guy yelled while slapping at Mack's cage. "Can't you quieten that bird, Grammy?" complained Daddy Guy.

"Now Guy, if you'd leave him alone, he'd leave you alone," explained Grammy. But that never happened. It was a constant battle between Mack and Daddy Guy.

When Daddy Guy was home, Mack spent a lot of time in his cage on the front porch. Mack loved to talk to the people as they walked down the sidewalk, and most people never even saw Mack. So they had no clue who was talking to them.

"Hey boy!" Mack yelled from his cage. The man turned around trying to locate the voice, but no luck.

"Hey boy, can't you talk?" asked Mack. The man was frightened by this time but still did not see Mack.

By the time Mack cried out again, "Hey Boy!" That man ran off lickety split—he was scared to death.

Mack wasn't always a little stinker, he also had a compassionate side. I can remember a day when Grammy was on a ladder cleaning the window blinds. She lost her balance and came tumbling down.

"Grammy—you okay Grammy?" Mack really loved Grammy.

"I'm okay, Mack," she replied. It was strange how Mack kept up with Grammy.

Mack also hung out in the kitchen, he kept company with Grammy as she cooked. They talked to each other all the time. Mack favored only a few people. He loved Grammy, of course, but he loved me too. You see, I had asthma and could not play with Cha-Cha because I would wheeze, so I decided Mack would be mine. Mack would even eat peanuts right out of my hand. But Mack did not like my sister, Paula. He once grabbed her dress as she walked past his cage. Paula avoided Mack as much as possible. She had Cha-Cha, and I thought of Mack as mine. I tried to help Grammy with Mack.

One morning, Grammy decided it was time to clean out Mack's cage. When Grammy opened the cage door, I guess she startled Mack, and he bit the tar out of her finger. Grammy was quite upset with Mack. She picked that cage up and took it outside. She propped the cage up on the picnic table and then went after the water hose. She hosed him down good. "Aye, Aye!" cried Mack.

"Mack a bad boy, Mack a bad boy," whined Mack. He knew he made Grammy mad.

That afternoon, Grammy got over her madness. She always did. In fact, Grammy rarely lost her temper. Grammy then opened the cage and let Mack climb on her arm. Grammy was rubbing Mack's head and trying to make Mack happy again. Then Cha-cha walked past them and growled. Oh my gosh, the commotion began. Mack flew off Grammy's arm and headed toward the bathroom. Cha-Cha was right behind him barking.

CRASH, BOOM, BANG! Things went everywhere. The bathroom was a mess. Paula grabbed Cha-Cha and Grammy went after Mack. He was hiding behind the toilet. Grammy scooped him up and put him into his cage. Grammy covered his cage with a cloth.

"Mack's been bad boy! Bad Boy! Mack a bad boy!" cried Mack. He remained in that covered cage for the rest of the day!

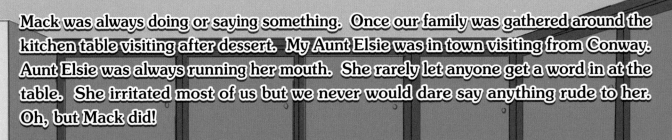

Mack was always doing or saying something. Once our family was gathered around the kitchen table visiting after dessert. My Aunt Elsie was in town visiting from Conway. Aunt Elsie was always running her mouth. She rarely let anyone get a word in at the table. She irritated most of us but we never would dare say anything rude to her. Oh, but Mack did!

"Aaah—shut up!" Mack screamed out. Our eyes lit up with surprise.

"Well.....I guess it's time to shut up when a bird tells you to," replied Aunt Elsie.

As time went on, Mack continued to get on my Daddy Guy's nerves.

"Bill, you must get rid of that bird. He is driving me crazy!" whined my grandfather to my dad.

As much as Grammy loved Mack, she knew how bad Mack was for Daddy Guy. She agreed to let my dad find Mack a new home. Mack was sent to live at a General store down the street. The owner of the store was a sweet old man, and Mack really seemed to like him. Mack loved talking to people at the store, but this was short lived.

The old man died and Mack had to then live with the man's wife. This lady was scared of Mack and kept his cage covered most of the time. This is very unhealthy for an Amazon parrot; they sometimes can get very depressed. Mack was very sad and rarely uttered a word anymore. Mack began to pluck out his feathers. He was bored with his dark life. I'm sure he missed the old man and Grammy too. The woman knew she had to get rid of Mack.

Over twenty years had passed since I last saw Mack. Our lives had gone on. Grammy and Daddy Guy no longer lived in that white frame home, but they did still have Cha-Cha. Paula and I had children of our own; Mack was just a sweet old memory of the past that we all shared stories about. We had no idea Mack was so miserable or even still alive. Then something really strange happened.

I was standing in line at Simmons Bank, and I heard this old lady complaining about this parrot she needed to get rid of. The lady felt sorry for the bird but knew it was awful how she never gave it attention. "What is your parrot's name?" I asked.

15

"Mack," she replied. My heart pounded.... Could this be our Mack? I then begged the woman to let me follow her home to pick Mack up. I called my dad and told him the whole story. We both went to the lady's home. There Mack was, all covered up. He looked like a frail skinny bird with hardly a feather. Mack was not the beautiful outspoken parrot anymore; I began to cry as the woman quickly agreed to let us have him.

My dad agreed to let me take Mack back to Grammy. Mack never uttered a word on our drive to Grammy and Daddy Guy's. I truly think Mack was very close to death. Would Mack remember Grammy? And Cha-Cha? Grammy just wept when she realized this parrot was Mack. When Mack heard Grammy's voice, he uttered, "GRAMMY!"

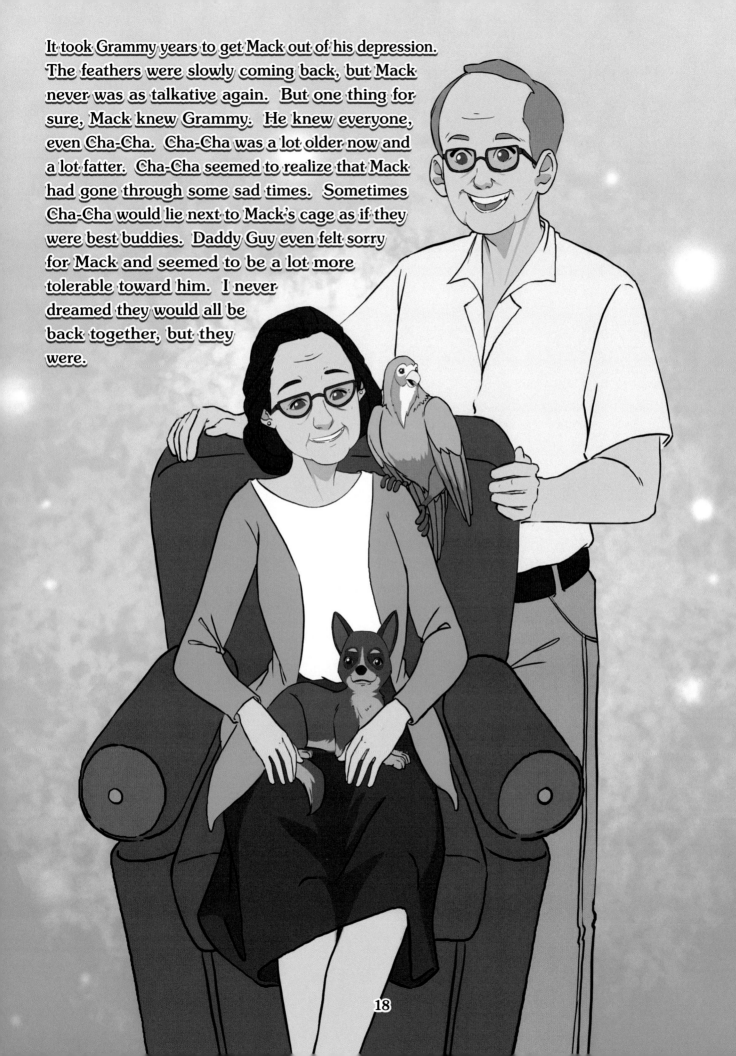

It took Grammy years to get Mack out of his depression. The feathers were slowly coming back, but Mack never was as talkative again. But one thing for sure, Mack knew Grammy. He knew everyone, even Cha-Cha. Cha-Cha was a lot older now and a lot fatter. Cha-Cha seemed to realize that Mack had gone through some sad times. Sometimes Cha-Cha would lie next to Mack's cage as if they were best buddies. Daddy Guy even felt sorry for Mack and seemed to be a lot more tolerable toward him. I never dreamed they would all be back together, but they were.

18